# Thistle

## and
## the Shell of Laughter

J. H. Sweet

Illustrated by Tara Larsen Chang

SOURCEBOOKS
Jabberwocky
AN IMPRINT OF SOURCEBOOKS

Published by Sourcebooks Jabberwocky, an imprint of Sourcebooks,
Inc.
P.O. Box 4410, Naperville, Illinois 60567-4410
(630) 961-3900
Fax: (630) 961-2168
www.fairychronicles.com

Cataloging in Publication data is on file with the publisher.

ISBN-13: 978-1-4022-0874-4
ISBN-10: 1-4022-0874-X

Printed and bound in the United States of America.
LB 10 9 8 7 6 5 4 3 2 1

*To Steve,*
*for laughter*

# MEET THE

## Thistle

NAME:
Grace Matthews

FAIRY NAME AND SPIRIT:
Thistle

WAND:
Porcupine Quill

GIFT:
Fierce and wild in
defending others

MENTOR:
Madam Robin

## Madam Robin

NAME:
Madam Robin

FAIRY NAME AND SPIRIT:
She is an enchanted robin

UNIQUE FACT:
She is the only Fairy Mentor
who is not a Fairy

GIFT:
Enchanted with the ability to
speak and long life

MENTOR TO:
Thistle

# FAIRY TEAM

## *Marigold*

NAME:
Beth Parish

FAIRY NAME AND SPIRIT:
Marigold

WAND:
Pussy Willow Branch

GIFT:
Can ward off nasty insects

MENTOR:
Aunt Evelyn,
Madam Monarch

## *Dragonfly*

NAME:
Jennifer Sommerset

FAIRY NAME AND SPIRIT:
Dragonfly

WAND:
Peacock Feather

GIFT:
Very fast and very agile

MENTOR:
Grandmother,
Madam Chrysanthemum

*Inside you is the power to do anything*

The Fairy Chronicles

**Come visit us at fairychronicles.com**

# Contents

# Chapter One

# Christmas Break

Grace Matthews was looking forward to a very exciting day. She was on Christmas break from school, along with her friends, Jennifer Sommerset and Beth Parish. The girls were spending three days at the home of Beth's Aunt Evelyn. With two whole weeks off from school, they would have plenty of time to work on holiday projects, visit with family, and participate in some very important, secret activities.

Grace and her friends were fairies. This meant that in addition to being regular nine-year-old girls, they also each had a fairy spirit. Grace was a thistle fairy. Jennifer had the fairy spirit of a red dragonfly. And Beth's spirit was that of a marigold.

Carrying out fairy activities was a lot of responsibility for young girls, but they handled themselves very well under the guidance of their fairy mentors. Most fairy mentors were older fairies. Beth's Aunt Evelyn was a monarch butterfly fairy. She was called Madam Monarch by other fairies and acted as Beth's mentor. Jennifer's mentor was her grandmother, a yellow chrysanthemum fairy called Madam Mum. But Grace's mentor was unique in the fairy realm—a very wise old robin. Madam Robin had been bewitched at one time and could speak.

Madam Robin had first appeared on Grace's bedroom windowsill when Grace was seven years old. After noticing the robin's recurring visits, Grace began to speak to the bird. When the robin actually

spoke back, Grace was not alarmed, she was delighted. She listened carefully to Madam Robin's instructions and learned quickly how to be a fairy. Under careful guidance, she learned how to take fairy form and how to fly.

Standard fairy form was six inches high. When in this form, fairies only appeared to look like their fairy spirits if regular people happened to see them. Grace's parents had never seen their daughter as a fairy, but if they had, she would have looked just like a tiny thistle wildflower.

From Madam Robin, Grace also learned about pixie dust and the fairy handbook. Pixie dust was carried by fairies in small pouches on their belts and was used to help them perform fairy magic. The fairy handbook was a small, fawn-colored book used as a source of information for fairies. In it, they found answers to fairy questions and guidance to make good fairy decisions.

The handbook also had the ability to age with its owner. Right now, Grace's handbook contained information that a nine-year-old could understand. As she got older, the information would become more complex, to help her make more mature decisions.

For two years, as Grace learned to be a fairy, her mom and dad heard frequent laughter from her room. Out of curiosity, they often checked on her. She was usually smiling and a little breathless, but they found nothing out of the ordinary. In the end, Mr. and Mrs. Matthews decided that they were so pleased to have a happy child, instead of a sad one, it didn't matter what she was laughing about in her room all by herself.

Grace had short, spiky blond hair and enormous gray eyes. In fairy form, she had tall, pointed, feathery gray wings and wore a pale purple dress made of prickly thistle petals that came to just above her knees.

Her fairy wand was an enchanted porcupine quill. Her first wand had been a strand of braided horsetail, but it was so full of horse enchantment that it was too strong for her. It nearly shook her arm off. So Madam Robin had arranged for a new wand, and it was meant to be. Grace and her porcupine quill were a perfect team.

Each fairy was given a special gift relating to her fairy spirit. Grace's gift was the ability to defend fiercely against attack. This had proven useful once when Grace had to face a pack of mean gremlins.

When Grace learned about her fairy gift, she begged her parents to let her take karate and fencing lessons. In karate, she learned many defensive maneuvers including how to block kicks and punches, and how to use leverage. Fencing

Thistle

taught Grace excellent foot coordination. And she could use her wand as a kind of sword to defend herself if attacked by nasty spirits like gremlins, or mean insects like hornets.

Grace also had a natural ability to stand up to bullies, if needed. In November, she helped a girl at school who was getting picked on by older kids. It wasn't so much fun anymore when the bigger kids realized that the little girl had a friend who was willing to stand up to them.

However, Grace also learned from Madam Robin that fairies were not allowed to use their fairy gifts for anything trivial, and younger fairies were never supposed to use fairy magic unless supervised by a fairy mentor. Grace never used any magic unless Madam Robin or another fairy mentor gave approval. And she had already learned how important it was for fairies not to abuse their power.

Jennifer was in Grace's class at school. She was a tall, thin, athletic black girl with very short, wavy dark hair. As a dragonfly fairy, Jennifer had dark red wings and wore a soft, red velvet fuzz dress. Her special fairy gift included speed and agility, and her wand was an enchanted peacock feather.

Beth lived on the opposite side of town and went to a different school. She had medium length, curly, golden brown hair. In fairy form, Beth wore a gold and yellow dress made of crinkly marigold petals. She also had pale gold wings and wore a crown of tiny marigold flowers. As her unique fairy gift, Beth was given the ability to ward off unfriendly insects because marigold flowers had bug-repelling qualities in nature. Beth's wand was a tiny pussy willow branch.

Grace's father worked for a computer manufacturer and was going to an out-of-town conference for three days. Beth's Aunt Evelyn offered to keep Grace so that Grace's mother could accompany him for a short vacation. Jennifer's grandmother, who usually watched Jennifer while her parents worked, wanted to travel to visit some friends for a few days. So she arranged for Jennifer to have a three-night sleepover at Aunt Evelyn's too. And Beth's mom and dad were happy to have Beth stay with her aunt for a few days so they would have time to finish their Christmas shopping and fix up the house for holiday company.

Aunt Evelyn picked up all three girls early in the morning and brought them to her house on Cherry Lane. The girls loved visiting Aunt Evelyn. Her house was a perfect fairy haven. It was the color of robin's egg blue and had tangerine colored trim.

The door of the house was bright red, and a grassy-green colored porch swing hung just to the left of the front steps. The inside of the house was full of fun, mixed-up colors too. A plum purple writing desk, hot pink throw rug, and mint green coat rack all sat just inside the front door. And the rest of the house was decorated in multicolored fashion as well.

In the afternoon, the fairies would be attending a special Christmas Fairy Circle. Fairy Circles were what fairies called their gatherings. Grace, Beth, and Jennifer had another good friend they usually spent a lot of time with, a firefly fairy named Lenox Hart. But she was traveling with her family to visit relatives for part of the holidays. They would miss her at the sleepover and at Fairy Circle.

While Jennifer and Beth were in the living room making Christmas decorations and playing cat's cradle and jacks, Grace went into the hallway to practice karate kicks and to pretend to block punches. But after a while, she got tired and went to help make decorations. Beth and Jennifer were stringing popcorn and cranberries on thread for garlands. Aunt Evelyn would use the strings of popcorn and cranberries to decorate her Christmas tree. Then after Christmas, she would hang the garlands out of her upstairs windows for the birds to eat.

As they worked, Grace told her friends, "I helped Brownie Stephen and Brownie William move last weekend. They had to find a more suitable family to live with."

Ordinarily, brownies and fairies didn't get along very well. Brownies were boy fairies, about seven inches high, and full of mischief. They liked to play pranks, especially on fairies. But Grace loved brownie mischief. Of all the fairies, she got along best with the brownies.

The fairies had met Brownie Stephen before. He was a red-haired, river stone brownie. Grace explained that William was Stephen's best friend, a moss brownie with black hair.

Brownies derived their fairy spirits from earthy things like acorns, pinecones, minerals, crystals, and mushrooms. They liked to live in regular people's houses and were usually very helpful. Brownies would clean up spills, fish out socks from behind dryers, organize toolboxes, untangle items in sewing cabinets, put up garden tools, clean out grass from under lawn mowers, straighten up kitchen drawers, and find missing items. These were some of their favorite things to do. However, brownies needed to be properly rewarded with pastries and milk.

Beth and Jennifer went on stringing cranberries and popcorn as Grace continued with her story. "The brownies had been living with the Blair family out on Pear Blossom Lane. Well, they weren't getting enough milk and pastries so they decided to move. But first, they went a little overboard on the pranks. For starters, they tangled up all of Mrs. Blair's yarn. Then they mismatched the socks in the sock drawers and short sheeted all of the beds."

Grace started laughing as she told of the pranks. "Then, they exchanged the salt with the pepper in the salt-and-pepper shakers." She was now laughing so hard that she started snorting, and her face turned very red. "And then...and then...." Grace fell out of her chair and onto the floor, rocking back and forth, hugging her knees. After a few moments, she finally caught her breath and finished her sentence. "And then...they unplugged everything."

As her friends giggled, Grace added a final comment. "Either the Blairs didn't realize they had brownies living with them, or they didn't care to keep them. I think it would be very useful to have a brownie or two living in the house." Jennifer and Beth nodded, but were secretly glad that neither of their homes had brownies. They were not fond of brownie tricks and didn't think their parents would be either.

After awhile, the girls took a break from making decorations to play a few games of Chinese jumprope. When they got tired of jumping, they went out onto the front porch to visit with Aunt Evelyn. Mr. Dusel, the garden gnome, was just coming up to the front steps. Like all garden gnomes, he was a dusty brown color all over, about ten inches high, and wore a bushy moustache. It was his job to help plants grow and add colors to the yard and garden as needed.

Aunt Evelyn and her orange cat, Maximillion, had been watching Mr. Dusel's progress this morning, and had both received a long lecture on mulching techniques from the knowledgeable gnome. Like most gnomes, he was extremely proud of his work and loved to share information.

Mr. Dusel especially loved working in the gardens and yards of houses occupied by fairies because they could see him and talk to him. To non-magical people, a gnome would look just like an ordinary object such as a watermelon, a football, or a tree stump. In fact, to the postman who had delivered mail a half-hour earlier, Mr. Dusel looked just like a round concrete steppingstone.

"Hello, girls," he said to them. Then Mr. Dusel addressed Aunt Evelyn. "I finished mulching the iris bed. It should be nice and cozy until spring. And I harvested the zinnia seeds. Are you ready with the envelopes, Evelyn?" he asked.

"Yes, here they are," Aunt Evelyn replied. Her zinnias had been so healthy and beautiful this year, she had let many of the flowers go to seed. She and Mr. Dusel would plant the seeds in the spring and hope for a showy bed next year too. After a nice cool fall, the flower heads were finally dried, and the seeds were ready for collection.

"And the envelopes please..." said Mr. Dusel, sounding much like a game show host. He put his hand into one of his pockets and pulled out a handful of seeds.

"Red…" he said. It seemed that each of the gnome's fifteen overall pockets, and his pant cuffs, held a different color of zinnia seeds. "Yellow, orange, light purple, white, pale pink, gold, off-white, hot pink, dark purple…."

When they finished filling and labeling the envelopes, Mr. Dusel added, "You might want to have the girls pull the dried stems and put them on the compost pile."

"Oh, I'll do it!" cried Jennifer, eagerly. It was part of a fairy's job to protect nature. Fairies took things like recycling and composting very seriously. However, Jennifer took her conservation and environmental concerns to a whole new level. She was the "Queen of Recycling" in her neighborhood, and had authored two brochures: *51 Ways to Reuse Coffee Cans* and *102 Uses for Butter Tubs*.

The butter tub brochure had just been finished and printed, and Jennifer was looking forward to distributing it at Fairy Circle this afternoon. She hoped her friends would be just as thrilled as she was about reusing plastic butter and margarine containers for things like molding sand for sandcastles, planting seasonal herbs, catching fish in fish tanks, freezing water to fill ice chests, and storing craft supplies.

When Jennifer returned from stacking the dried zinnia stalks on the compost pile, the three girls presented Mr. Dusel with one of the Christmas ornaments they had constructed. It was made with cranberries strung on wire, then bent into a star shape and tied with a dark green satin ribbon for hanging.

The gnome was very pleased and thanked the girls earnestly. "This is wonderful. My wife loves the color of cranberries. And it will fit perfectly on our front door."

Mr. Dusel lived in a dugout-style house on the side of a long hill on Peach Tree Ridge. The hill hosted a large gnome

Mr. Dusel

community, and Mr. Dusel had many gnome neighbors. Since his gnome door was only about a foot high, the Christmas ornament would be the perfect size for a door decoration. He said goodbye to the girls and left, carrying the ornament gift carefully away with him on his arm like a handbag.

# Fairy Circle

They set off at eleven o'clock to go to Fairy Circle. The girls all piled into Aunt Evelyn's lime green station wagon and buckled up. Then they sang Christmas carols to pass the time on the trip. When they got tired of singing, they talked about fairy things like doves and toadstool rings.

About thirty minutes later, after a bumpy ride down several remote country roads, the fairies arrived in a dense area of woods. Aunt Evelyn parked on the side of a dirt road. With four little *pops*, they all changed into fairy form and flew up a hill and through a bit of woods to reach the Fairy Circle. In honor of Christmas, the fairies were meeting under a pine tree today. The low-hanging evergreen branches would shield them from the crisp December winds.

Madam Toad was the leader of the fairies for this region and had chosen this Fairy Circle site very carefully. The pine tree was just on the edge of a small apple farm. Unicorns were drawn to apple trees, and Madam Toad hoped that the fairies would be treated to a unicorn visit at some point during the afternoon.

The fairy leader had arrived early and had decorated the underside of the pine boughs with hanging cranberries. Then, using her miniature red rosebud-stem wand, she had enchanted the cranberries to make them glow softly.

As the Fairy Circle began, Dragonfly helped Madam Toad light a fire in a fairy fire shield, which was a shallow iron bowl made especially for fairy campfires. The shield protected the earth from being scarred by the fire. Many of the fairies whispered the words, "*Fairy light*," to make the tips of their wands glow softly. Then they placed their wands in convenient spots around the circle to help add merry light to the gathering.

The Christmas Fairy Circle had been planned far enough in advance so that many fairies were able to attend. This included Madam Shrew and Milkweed, two fairies from the far North region.

Madam Shrew and Milkweed were friends with several troll families who lived in their area. The trolls generally got along well with the fairies and had baked special pumpkin cookies as a holiday troll friendship offering for Madam Shrew and Milkweed to take with them to the Fairy Circle. The only problem was that trolls often had trouble remembering things, and they had left out some of the key ingredients of the pumpkin cookie recipe, so the cookies tasted a little funny. But it was a nice gesture and very gratefully received by the fairies.

For the first time, the fairies at the circle got to meet Starfish. She was a coastal fairy. Madam Toad had coordinated her visit with Madam Oyster, the leader of the Gulf region fairies. There weren't very many fairies in the Gulf area, so this was a special treat for Starfish. Madam Oyster was unable to attend but had arranged for a whooping crane to bring Starfish to the Fairy Circle.

Starfish's name was Gina. She had long, curly blond hair and wore a soft, sand colored, star-shaped cap. Her dress fell to just below her knees and was made of sweeping, green and blue tendrils that looked like brightly colored seaweed strands. Starfish's tiny, delicate wings were the exact color of sea foam. When she moved, a refreshing mist of sea drops lightly sprayed the other fairies. And her voice had a rich, breathless quality like coastal winds and roaring waves. Starfish carried a sea urchin spine for her wand.

Thistle, Dragonfly, and Marigold thought Starfish was the most beautiful fairy they had ever seen. But they had thought this about Milkweed when they first met her too. All fairies were beautiful, even Madam Toad, so it was probably just the excitement of meeting a new fairy that made them so enchanted with Starfish.

The girls visited with many other friends as well including Periwinkle, Spiderwort, Tulip, Lily, Primrose, Magnolia, Carnation, Morning Glory, and Rosemary. There was also an older butterfly fairy that they had not seen before, but Madam Toad obviously knew her. Her spirit was that of a spicebush swallowtail butterfly. Madam Swallowtail's velvety black wings were very large with glowing ivory eyespots, and her silky dress was black with a bluish sheen. Madam Monarch spent a lot of time talking to her. Together, they looked very regal.

Madam Robin was also present and spent much of her time singing Christmas tunes with her beautiful birdsong voice.

Brownie Alan had also been invited to Fairy Circle. He was a mushroom brownie with messy, light brown hair. He was dressed in the traditional soft tan colors of the brownies and wore a mushroom-shaped cap on his head.

Alan had spent the last six months as the keeper of the Feather of Hope, which was the source of all hope on earth. He had ridden on birds and animals, and even a few dolphins and whales, to spread hope all over the world. He was no longer on feather duty and was now able to take a well-deserved break. Alan spent most of his time at the Fairy Circle talking to Marigold. After meeting her over the summer, he had been keeping in touch with her through nut messages.

Nut messages were hollowed-out nuts that the fairies used to send notes and letters back and forth to one another. Birds and animals liked to deliver them for the fairies.

When Thistle and Dragonfly came over to say hi to Alan, Marigold told them, "Alan was telling me about his meteorite collection. By the time meteors hit the earth to become meteorites, they are usually only about the size of peas and marbles, so they are perfect for collecting. Aunt Evelyn is going to take us meteorite hunting next week. I think I'll start a collection too."

Alan shuffled his feet and stuffed his hands into his pockets as Thistle and Dragonfly expressed polite interest. He was pleased when they moved off because he was somewhat shy and preferred to talk to Marigold alone. As Dragonfly and Thistle left, Alan smiled sheepishly and told Marigold, "I played three pranks this morning to get it out of my system, so everyone here is safe." When he said this, Marigold giggled and blushed.

Thistle spent some time helping Dragonfly pass out her butter tub brochures. Then they helped set up for refreshments. Since the fairies had plenty of time to prepare, there was quite a spread. They had their usual fairy fare of powdered sugar puff pastries, raspberries, peanut butter and marshmallow créme sandwiches, homemade fudge, and lemon jellybeans. But they also had caramel popcorn balls, candy cane crunch

cookies, bread and butter pickles, cherry chip loaf, tiny pecan pies, and roasted yams. And they drank hot cider and cocoa from acorn cap cups.

Madam Toad had also created a special, additional Christmas treat–snowflake fairy divinity.  It was sweet, creamy, and fluffy like regular divinity, but was made into the shapes of snowflakes for the season.  The candies were also enchanted by Madam Toad to float and fly around the Fairy Circle. So the fairies enjoyed their refreshments with snowflake fairy divinity hovering and swirling all about them. They made sure to pack up a large quantity of the snowflake divinity for Madam Shrew and Milkweed to take back as a gift for their troll friends.

While they were visiting, just as Madam Toad had hoped, two unicorns approached the pine tree. The fairies were delighted. The unicorns' brilliant white coats glistened,

and their golden horns flashed with the light of the afternoon sun. They acknowledged the fairies with nods of their heads. Madam Toad had brought several apples with her since the apple orchard was bare this time of year. She enchanted them to roll out to the unicorns. The fruit was very happily accepted.

The unicorns munched contentedly while gazing at the fairies with warm, golden brown eyes. After they finished their treat, the unicorns lingered for a few moments while the fairies flitted around them. But they didn't stay long. As soon as all of the fairies had had a chance to see them up close, and wish them holiday greetings, the unicorns galloped away, their snowy-white tails and manes rippling in the afternoon breezes. Even though they hadn't stayed long, it was a real treat to see unicorns.

Next, the fairies all exchanged friendship bracelets that they had made. Many of the girls had brought extra bracelets as gifts for the visitors. Marigold had made a special one for Alan in honor of their friendship. It was tan, brown, gold, and yellow—the exact colors of mushrooms and marigold flowers combined.

When nearly everyone had finished eating and exchanging gifts, an elf joined the group. He was a little over two feet tall and had to stoop to fit under the pine tree branches. The visitor had dark hair, hazel eyes, and was dressed in olive and brown clothes with a soft, dark green cap on his head. He also had a long, clear crystal shard hanging from a silky brown cord around his neck.

While they waited for Madam Toad to introduce the guest, Thistle looked up elves in her fairy handbook:

*Elves: Elves are happy, implike magical beings. They are generally good-natured practical jokers, though not as mischievous as brownies. Elves look young, but most are actually very old. They have lived on the earth longer than any other magical creatures and cannot grow old or die. Elf magic is something of a mystery. Elves do not often use their magic in front of other beings, so it is not known how far their abilities extend. It is clear that they can appear and disappear at will, and they are considered to be the most powerful of all magical creatures.*

Thistle didn't think their elf visitor fit the description in the handbook very closely since instead of smiling, he was frowning and looking more serious than any creature she had ever seen. She couldn't imagine anyone being so serious this time of year. The elf didn't look like elves she had seen in picture books either. His ears were barely pointed, and he did not have a pointy hat or shoes. Instead, he looked rather like a large brownie.

Next, Madam Toad called the Fairy Circle meeting to order. The fairy leader looked magnificent. She wore a crown of tiny red rosebuds to match her wand and had small, sparkling, dark green wings perched on her plump shoulders. The underskirt and sleeves of her dress were a muddy, greenish-brown color; but her pale green overskirt and bodice were laden with shimmering moisture drops, which glistened like jewels from the soft light under the pine boughs.

Madam Toad's voice was very deep and loud, commanding everyone's attention. "Welcome! Happy Christmas, Hanukkah, and Kwanzaa! We have a special guest with us today. This is Staid. He has come to ask for our help."

Staid sat down beside Madam Toad in order to not have to stand stooping under the pine boughs. "Hello," he said, nodding to them. If possible, he looked even more serious than he had a minute ago, and his frown deepened as he addressed them. "The Shell of Laughter has been stolen."

The younger fairies all looked at one another, not really understanding, as the elf went on. "For over one hundred years, I have been the protector of the Shell of Laughter. It is my job to distribute laughter over the earth using the jet stream, trade winds, Zephyrs, and other winds. I have not yet reported this to Mother Nature. But I need to get the shell back quickly. I only have two days to catch the tail end of a trade wind. If I miss it, there will be no laughter in Iceland, Norway, Sweden, and Finland for an entire year."

The fairies all looked at each other, wide-eyed and afraid. Thistle was especially horrified. She couldn't imagine any place without laughter. Her mouth open and her eyes even larger than normal, she leaned forward, hanging on Staid's every word as he continued. "Laughter and tears must both exist, but in balance with each other. My twin brother, Blithe, is the protector of the Stone of Tears. I have contacted him. The stone is safe, so this is not a double plot as I feared at first."

Staid paused and sighed, frowning even more deeply. "My home is not far from here. The shell only disappeared last night so it is probably still close by. But I need help tracking it down quickly."

Then Madam Toad again addressed the fairies. "I have decided that Thistle will lead this mission. She is the most full of laughter of any fairy I have ever encountered. And quite frankly, she would have the most to lose if the shell is not found. Madam Robin will supervise," Madam

Toad added. "She is very familiar with the woods and knows many of the forest creatures. Marigold and Dragonfly will accompany them."

The fairies all said goodbye to one another and wished each other happy holidays as the Fairy Circle was breaking up. Madam Shrew and Milkweed departed with their friendship bracelets and divinity on the large hawk that had brought them. And Starfish flew away on the whooping crane to make the journey back to the Gulf. The rest of the fairies wished Thistle, Dragonfly, Marigold, and Madam Robin good luck as they prepared to leave with Staid.

Madam Monarch told the young fairies, "I will check in with your parents regularly and tell them you are doing fine. Be careful." With that, she hugged each of the girls and flew off through the bit of woods and down the hill to where she had parked the car.

# Chapter Three

# The Elf's Cave

As the fairies and Madam Robin traveled with Staid through the woods, he told them more about his job. "I have only made one mistake in a hundred years. I caught the same trade wind twice and distributed double the laughter in Mexico. It was not a good thing. People were laughing at funerals, at solemn church services, and at very serious tragic play performances. I had to meet with Mother Nature to explain."

Staid shivered a little and went on. "She was in undertow form when I talked to her.

Even though I can't drown or die, it was still very frightening."

The fairies nodded understandingly, and Madam Robin chirped sympathetically. None of them had ever met Mother Nature. She was the guardian of magical creatures and supervisor of all nature activities. Mother Nature was very busy, extremely powerful, and was often in dangerous forms such as blizzard, earthquake, and lightning. No one could ever know when she would be in a safe form like cloud, rainbow, or mist.

As she flew alongside Madam Robin, Thistle looked up the Shell of Laughter in her fairy handbook. She read the entry aloud to Dragonfly and Marigold who were close by:

" *The Shell of Laughter:*
*The Shell of Laughter is the source of all laughter on earth. It is actually a factory that produces laughter, like a manufacturing plant. Inside, the shell is divided into sections called chambers. Each chamber contains a key ingredient or component of laughter. The components of laughter include the following: buried treasure, the sound of puppies barking, a two-part joke, bubbles, Christmas snow, soprano wind chimes, eighteen tickle feathers, and birdsong."*

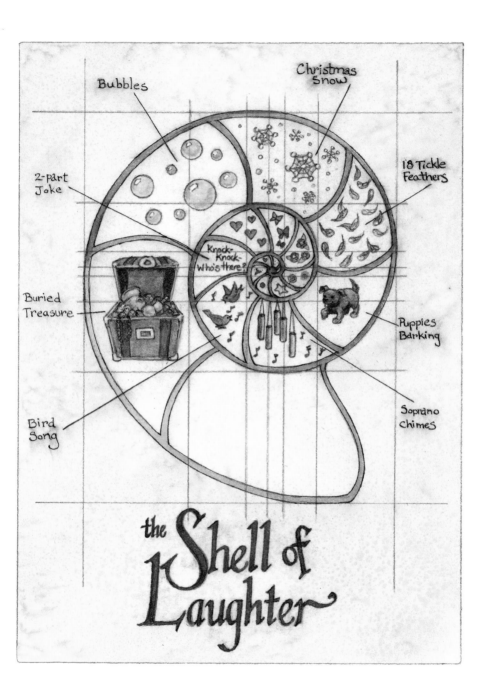

Bubbles

Christmas Snow

18 Tickle Feathers

2-part Joke

Knock-Knock-Who's there?

Buried Treasure

Puppies Barking

Bird Song

Soprano Chimes

the Shell of Laughter

The fairies and Madam Robin all smiled, delighted to learn what laughter was made of. But Staid didn't smile. He simply frowned and stared. Then he frowned some more. It seemed he took his job so seriously that he never smiled. In fact, he had not smiled or laughed for over one hundred years.

Staid's home was a cave in a dark, almost scary part of the forest. It seemed odd that the Shell of Laughter was kept in such a dark, foreboding place.

However, the cave itself was quite different than the forest surrounding it. Inside, the main chamber glittered brightly with colored minerals and crystals. There was a single flickering candle in one corner, and the glow from this tiny flame was enough to set the entire cave alight with brilliant sparkles from the prism effect of crystals reflecting the light. In another corner of the cave, a soft silver cloth lay on top of a flat stalagmite.

Staid's Crystal Cave

"This is where the shell is usually kept," said Staid.

Suddenly, the cave was filled with high-pitched, echoing giggles, and a small hedgehog appeared from behind a stone. He snorted and giggled happily when he saw Staid. As Staid approached him, the hedgehog curled up and rolled onto his back, exposing his soft pink underbelly. Staid tickled him, and the hedgehog's giggles became a fit of giggles as he rolled around the floor.

Over and over again, he rolled back and forth across the length of the cave, sniggering and giggling. When he finally stopped rolling around, Staid said, "This is Snickers."

Thistle moved forward to speak to the hedgehog. "You know, a prickle is very much like a tickle." Immediately, the hedgehog rolled onto his back. When Thistle prickled his tummy, he had another fit of giggles that turned into snickers and snorting.

Laughing happily, Thistle rolled around on the floor with Snickers. The other fairies couldn't help but laugh too.

Then they all sat down while Staid told them about the theft of the shell. "Either Snickers or myself is here at all times, so we can't understand how this happened. The last time we saw the shell was around nine o'clock last night. I was consulting my schedule." Staid gestured to a round rock table in the center of the cave, filled with large sheets of paper that looked like charts. He explained further. "The laughter is spread by many different winds, some of them connecting with each other to continue their journey to specific destinations.

"I follow a very complex schedule made up by Mother Nature each year based on the trade winds, when the Chinook will start south, siroccos, if there is going to be a typhoon, when the monsoons begin, tornado activity, and other seasonal factors that affect wind. At about nine-thirty, I had finished confirming my schedule for the week. When I turned around, the shell was gone. I was sitting facing the entrance to the cave. No one could have entered or left without my noticing them."

Before the fairies or Madam Robin could comment or ask any questions, there was a knock at the cave entrance. "That will be Tom," said Staid.

Tom was a leprechaun and was Staid's friend. He was about eight inches high and had light brown hair. Tom looked very robust and was dressed entirely in orange. The fairies very quickly looked up leprechauns in their handbooks:

*Leprechauns: Leprechauns are small magical beings with the ability to steal and find treasure. They are very clever and love riddles. They also like daring others to find treasure they have hidden. However, leprechauns sometimes hide treasure so cleverly that even they cannot find it again once they have hidden it. Like elves, leprechauns have the ability to appear and disappear at will. They can also fly without wings. It is unknown how they accomplish this; but it is believed that their powers come from a mag-ical shamrock kept in their pocket, which gives them the ability to fly and perform other magic.*

Staid introduced Tom to the fairies and Madam Robin.

After a quick hello, Tom turned to Staid. "I just got your message, and I've come to help."

The leprechaun and the elf had become friends while searching for one of Tom's hidden treasures. Tom had met Staid in the woods and had dared him to find a treasure he had hidden. Then, when the elf couldn't find it, they had searched together. Tom was an excellent treasure tracker, but he was an even cleverer treasure hider. It had taken them nearly two years to find the treasure Tom had hidden.

"This is wonderful," said Staid. "Since one of the key components of the Shell of Laughter is buried treasure, you will be a tremendous asset to our team." He paused before going on. "I think the best way to start would be to ask some of our neighbors if they have seen or heard anything suspicious lately."

Since it was getting late and dark, the group decided not to set off until morning. Staid gave them all supper, which was simply soup and bread. But it was very flavorful and satisfying since it was made with elf magic. He made up soft beds in one corner of the cave for his guests. Then he nicely, but firmly, asked Snickers to hold any more giggles until morning. The only thing the fairies heard that night was Snicker's light snoring and a few soft dream giggles.

# Chapter Four

# The Gnome,
# the Bobolink, and the Witch

The party set out at dawn after a breakfast of toast and marmalade. The elf led them through the woods in search of his closest neighbor, a wood gnome named Mr. Ambertoes. Staid explained that wood gnomes lived in tree houses, but Mr. Ambertoes would have already left his house for the day so they would have to look for him on his work route.

"He colors the crystals and minerals in my cave," Staid told them, "but I'm not expecting him until next Thursday."

Staid had a pretty good idea of Mr. Ambertoes' work route. He first led the group to an old oak tree. Looking around the ground by the trunk, he told the others, "I thought he might be harvesting and planting some of these acorns, but he hasn't been here."

Tom approached the oak tree as the others moved off. A short distance away, they all turned to stare at the leprechaun. Tom was stamping his foot and shouting at the tree. He caught up with them a few moments later, a little breathless.

"The tree wouldn't give me a riddle," Tom explained in a frustrated voice. "But I guess the yelling didn't help convince him much," he added, a little embarrassed for having lost his temper.

Oak trees could see the future. But they never gave out direct information or advice. Instead, they liked to give others complex riddles. Evidently, this oak did not want to share information at all with the leprechaun.

They found Mr. Ambertoes at their next stop. He was hard at work adding color to the berries covering a clump of holly bushes. The wood gnome was about the same size as a garden gnome, but he had a beard and was dressed all in green. Even his skin had a bit of a greenish look. Staid introduced the fairies and Madam Robin to Mr. Ambertoes; but before Staid could explain why they were there, he and Tom suddenly disappeared with a sound like little metallic *clicks*.

"Where did they go?" asked Thistle.

Madam Robin flew up to a high branch in a nearby chinaberry tree. As she did this, Snickers scurried behind a tree trunk, and the fairies heard a jingling of bells. Two hikers, a man and a woman, suddenly appeared through the trees.

"We are near a hiking trail," Mr. Ambertoes whispered.

Mr. Ambertoes

The fairies kept very still as the hikers passed. The man and woman had strings of bells hanging from their backpacks. They didn't notice Mr. Ambertoes, who would have looked like a smooth gray stone to them, or the fairies huddled next to him.

Thistle and Marigold were very thankful not to be noticed. Since marigold and thistle flowers rarely bloomed in December, they would have drawn too much attention from an observant hiker, or a flower enthusiast.

After the hikers had passed, Staid and Tom returned.

Marigold asked the others, "Why would they wear bells? It doesn't seem very smart to make so much noise while hiking in the woods."

Mr. Ambertoes answered her. "It's actually very smart. They wear the bells to give animals plenty of time to get out of their way. They are less likely to surprise a bear or a mountain lion if they make noise. Animals that are startled can be dangerous."

Staid then explained to Mr. Ambertoes about the disappearance of the Shell of Laughter, and asked the gnome if he had seen anything unusual lately.

Mr. Ambertoes shook his head, but said that he would keep watch and send a message if he noticed anything. "I'll ask my neighbors, Mr. Quartzcork and Mr. Jasperwing, if they have seen or heard anything strange," he added.

As the group left him, Mr. Ambertoes quickly went back to work coloring holly berries.

"Next we'll try a family of trolls that lives nearby," Staid told them. "Since they can't come into the sunlight, I'll talk to them in the dark of their den. They won't be happy about waking up, but this is important."

However, the group didn't get as far as the trolls' den. A small bird flitting from branch to branch beside them began twittering excitedly to draw their attention. "*Bobo-LINK-en, bobo-LINK-en*," he said.

As the bird continued his strange call, Madam Robin told the group, "It's a bobolink bird." She flew to the branch that the bobolink rested on and added her own chirps and twitters of bird conversation, explaining their mission to the new arrival. When the bobolink again sang his strange song, Madam Robin said, "He wants to show me something important. I'll be right back." With that, they flew away together.

Five minutes later they were back, and Madam Robin said laughing, "It's nothing to do with the Shell of Laughter. He wanted to show me his family. They had a late brood this year, and the youngsters are still learning to fly." The bobolink nodded proudly.

But as the fairy group started on their way, the bobolink's song became louder. "*Bobo-LINK-en, bobo-LINK-en!*" He moved his head forward and back quickly, like a woodpecker, but without a tree to peck.

Madam Robin said to him, "I'm sorry, we haven't got time for a longer visit."

Thistle was watching the bird closely. "He's pointing," she said. The bobolink nodded at her, then did his woodpecker impression again, pointing his beak a little to the left of the group. In the direction he pointed, they saw a tiny wisp of smoke visible through the tops of the trees.

"Of course," said Staid. "Matilda." The bobolink nodded again.

The elf thanked the bird, and once again the group set off through the trees as Staid explained, "Matilda is a friend of mine. She's a witch."

They hurried quickly through the woods to a small clearing and found Matilda sweeping her front porch steps. She was a plump little witch with a kindly expression, and she wore a dark blue dress with red shoes. The fairies thought Matilda looked slightly like a troll, mainly because she was only about four feet tall and was rather round. She had a large nose, and her gray hair was swept into a bun on top of her head. Around her neck, Matilda wore a string of dark purple hawthorn berries; and she had a daisy stuck behind one ear.

She said hello to them all as Staid introduced her. He declined her invitation for black root tea and told her the reason for their visit.

After thinking for a few moments, Matilda said, "Oh dear." She looked at the ground, then at each of their faces, then back at the ground. Wringing her hands,

the Witch
Matilda

the witch finally spoke again. "Oh dear, oh dear, oh dear!"

"What is it?" demanded Tom, impatiently.

Matilda propped her broom against the front door and sat down on the wooden steps. She shook her head and sighed before telling her story. "Three days ago, I sold Killjoy Crosspatch a ten-minute invisibility seed. Well, I traded actually. He had a bit of blue moon clover, which is very rare. It only grows during the most rare type of blue moon, and only the Black Stag can find it. I never would have been able to get blue moon clover any other way." She shook her head again sadly, giving Staid a stricken look.

Staid told the fairies and Madam Robin, "Killjoy Crosspatch is the Spirit of Sorrow. With an invisibility seed, he could have come into my cave at any time and taken the shell. This explains what happened."

Matilda looked worriedly at them. "I never thought he would do something this dreadful. I'm so sorry."

"Never mind," said Staid. "Do you know where we might find him?"

Matilda frowned as she answered. "Not many people go looking for Killjoy Crosspatch. He usually seeks out others. You must follow the Trail of Sorrow." She thought for a few moments and added, "If I wanted to find him, I would start in the darkest place." She looked around her little clearing and pointed to a dark shadow between two cedar trees. "I would start there," she told them. "The Trail of Sorrow will be well marked with sadness and grief."

The group said goodbye to Matilda and left swiftly.

# Chapter Five

# The Trail of Sorrow

The point between the two cedar trees led to the darkest part of the forest they had yet seen. Following dark shadows, the group had traveled for almost an hour when they heard a soft weeping. Hunting around for the source of the noise, Snickers discovered a small rabbit huddled under a bush. With Staid, Tom, and Snickers all peeking in under the bush, the fairies and Madam Robin flew in and surrounded the rabbit. The tiny creature was crying and sobbing, full of despair, as though something terrible had happened.

Madam Robin spoke to the rabbit in soft, soothing tones, trying to comfort her. Then Thistle and Dragonfly tried to ask her what was wrong. The tiny, shivering rabbit just shook her head and continued to sob.

Marigold sprinkled a little pixie dust on her and said, "*Be happy.*" But the rabbit went on weeping.

Thistle thought for a moment, then spoke. "We are on the Trail of Sorrow, and we have come across a very sorrowful little rabbit." The others in the group didn't say anything but looked questioningly at her. Thistle's brow crinkled, and her eyebrows came together with intense thinking. "What is the cure for sorrow?" she asked. Then in answer to her own question, Thistle said, "Laughter is medicine. The rabbit needs laughter as medicine."

With this, Thistle flew swiftly to Snickers who quickly flipped over onto his back and allowed Thistle to tickle his belly.

Instantly, the forest was filled with his loud giggles and snickers. Marigold, Dragonfly, and Tom started laughing just listening to him.

After a minute or so, the rabbit stopped crying, and a dark, greenish-gray cloud rose from her. The *Spell of Sorrow* had lifted. When Snickers kept giggling, the dark cloud trembled and shook, and began to lose its shape. Eventually, it broke apart, and wisps of the cloud drifted away in different directions.

Madam Robin praised Thistle and Snickers. "Wonderful! Good work!"

And Staid added, "Good job."

Tom, Marigold, and Dragonfly were nodding and smiling. Thistle and Snickers looked pleased. The tiny rabbit approached Snickers and rubbed her nose against his. He turned as pink as his tummy. Then the rabbit hopped away, a little embarrassed herself.

As they traveled farther into the eerie forest, through deeper and darker shadows, the fairies lit their wands for light.

"I sure wish Firefly were here," said Marigold.

Staid cupped his crystal necklace in his hands and spoke softly to it. As he let it fall against his chest, the pendant shimmered softly with light. The extra glow was very comforting to the fairies and Madam Robin.

As the fairies flew along, they came across a ring of toadstools. "Look!" cried Thistle, wide-eyed. "Remember what Madam Monarch told us about toadstool rings. They usually appear in places where fairies have been meeting." The group paused as Thistle looked up toadstool rings in her handbook and read the entry aloud to them:

*"Toadstool Rings: They are usually found in places where fairies have had a gathering. Toadstool*

rings tempt people, who are hoping to see fairies, back to the same spot over and over again. However, non-magical people cannot see fairies; and fairies seldom meet in the same place twice, so it is somewhat silly to return to a toadstool ring in the hopes of glimpsing fairies. Toadstool rings are thought to be bad omens by people who mistrust fairies."

"Maybe it's not so silly to look for fairies around toadstool rings," said Dragonfly. "After all, there are fairies here now." Thistle, Marigold, and Dragonfly quickly looked around them, almost expecting to see people hopefully watching the toadstool ring for signs of fairies.

The group had traveled for another hour when they heard crying again. This time, it was much louder. A large elk was sobbing with utter misery, as though he had just lost his best friend, twice. And there was such a state of gloom surrounding him that everyone in the group stayed well back, afraid of catching the sadness.

Again, Thistle and Snickers did their tickle laugh routine. This time, it took a little longer, since the elk was rather large. But the duo was persistent.

Finally, after several minutes of giggles and laughter, a dark, greenish-gray cloud rose from the elk, broke apart, and drifted away. As the cloud lifted, the elk stopped sobbing and looked at them with large, grateful eyes. He pawed at the ground with one of his front hooves, unearthing several acorns, which he pushed toward the fairies as a thank-you gesture. Then he walked proudly away towards a lighter, less gloomy part of the woods.

# Chapter Six

# Killjoy Crosspatch

The Trail of Sorrow was not hard to follow. The company simply kept to the darkest shadows. As they traveled along, the fairies flew closer to Tom. They had never met a leprechaun before and were very curious about him. His hand was in his jacket pocket as he flew.

Dragonfly asked slyly, "Can we see your magic shamrock?"

Tom turned his head with a jerk to look at her. "How did you know about that?" he asked.

"My handbook told me," she replied.

**TOM**
the Leprechaun

He smiled as he answered her question. "No, I have to keep it hidden or it will lose its magic."

"I thought all leprechauns wore green," said Marigold.

Tom answered a little indignantly. "I can wear any color I like." As he said this, his clothes magically changed from orange to bright purple, then back to orange again. He winked at the girls, and the fairies laughed in delight.

"And I thought all leprechauns had red hair," Thistle added.

"No one in my family has red hair," Tom answered. "But my mother's hair is blue," he added with twinkling eyes. With this, his hair turned from light brown to bright yellow, very briefly, before returning to brown again. The girls giggled at this entertainment. By now, the fairies were thoroughly enchanted with their new friend.

The colors of the forest became even deeper and blacker as they journeyed. The next evidence of sorrow they came upon was a tortoise that seemed consumed by grief. He was sobbing in agony and desperation, as though possessed by some terrible misfortune.

Again, Thistle and Snickers dosed out their laughter medicine, and the tortoise was relieved of the *Spell of Sorrow.*

As they continued to travel, the fairies were surprised when Tom suddenly flew off. He returned a few moments later, happily holding a very old looking coin. "I caught a glint of this through the trees," he said. Then he looked at them all apologetically and added, "I know. This isn't what I'm supposed to be looking for." But he carefully tucked the coin into his back trouser pocket and whistled a little tune as they went on ahead.

Thistle moved closer to fly next to Staid

as they continued their journey. "Why don't you ever smile?" she asked him timidly. She was afraid that she was being rude by asking him something this personal.

Staid didn't seem to mind the question and answered, "I am a balance to the shell. Someone full of laughter and happiness would not be able to withstand the effects of long-term exposure to the Shell of Laughter.

"My job is very complicated, and the timing has to be exact. Sometimes there is a connection of seven or eight winds to carry laughter to a single, designated spot. If the first wind of the chain is missed, the result could be a disaster—like no laughter in Canada and Alaska for an entire year. There is actually very little time for laughter in my schedule. If I weren't serious all of the time, I might make mistakes."

Staid paused a moment before going on. "But I guess the real answer to your question is that I was born with this personality. I was

Staid

chosen especially for this job because of my
serious and stoic personality. My twin
brother, Blithe, was born with a very bubbly,

happy personality. That is why he was chosen as protector of the Stone of Tears. He is
a balance to the stone and is able to carry out

his duties. A sad, woeful person would not be able to withstand exposure to the stone for very long. The Shell of Laughter and the Stone of Tears exist to balance each other, just as Blithe and I balance each other."

Suddenly, their conversation was interrupted with a shout from Tom. "We're getting close! I can smell buried treasure a mile away!"

Sure enough, after a few minutes, they came to a small, circular clearing in the woods. This was the darkest part of their journey so far. Black clouds seemed to hang just above their heads, as though waiting to descend and cover them, and a stringy gray mist swirled slowly through the air.

The clearing was filled with dark gray stones covered by a kind of thick moss. The shaggy moss was such a dark green that it looked almost black.

In the very center of the clearing, on the largest stone, sat Killjoy Crosspatch. The fairies hadn't noticed him at first because he blended in with the dark and gloom, and the color of the rocks.

The Spirit of Sorrow was about the same size as Staid, but he didn't have a distinct shape. It seemed he was partly made of the same dark, greenish-gray clouds of the spells that had covered the rabbit, elk, and tortoise. He was almost a pea green color, mottled with the dark, greenish-gray color. The spirit's arms, legs, and face seemed to be dripping and running, as though he were struggling to keep his shape. And he had large, pea green eyes that were sunk deep into his runny face.

The Spirit of Sorrow stared at them without speaking. Thistle, Marigold, and Dragonfly thought he was the most disgusting and foul creature they had ever seen.

"Where is the shell?" demanded Staid.

Killjoy Crosspatch didn't speak. Instead, a wide, uneven smile crept across his ugly face, and he slowly raised his hands in front of him. From his dripping palms, a dark gray, smoky cloud began to seep. It slowly crept towards the elf, the hedgehog, the leprechaun, Madam Robin, and the fairies.

They tried to take cover behind several of the rocks, but the oozing darkness followed them. It seemed there was no escape from the cloud of sorrow.

# Chapter Seven

# Mirth, Merriment,
## Joy, and Glee

The dark cloud covered the travelers, choking and smothering them. And it carried with it every unhappy thought they had ever had and every pain they had ever felt. The agony and misery of the cloud of despair cut deeply into them. Snickers curled up tightly against Staid's feet, whimpering. Madam Robin huddled next to Thistle, Marigold, and Dragonfly as she frantically tried to think of a way to protect the young fairies. But she was frozen in horror. She had never felt such unhappiness and despair. The fairies were shaking uncontrollably and crying. Tom had been knocked flat on his back and was staring into the blackness with a terrified look on his face.

Through her tears, Thistle pointed her wand at Killjoy Crosspatch and sobbed, "*R-Reflect! M-M-irror!*" But her spell was not strong enough to deflect the smothering cloud of sorrow.

Staid seemed the least affected of the group, but was still doubled up, holding his stomach in pain. With a tremendous effort, he reached out for Snickers and tickled him. A small giggle was heard in the clearing. As Staid kept on tickling Snickers, the giggling grew louder, and Thistle joined in with the happiness of hearing the hedgehog laugh.

With the sound of laughter, Killjoy Crosspatch was pushed backwards off of his stone, and the cloud of sorrow lifted slightly.

However, it seemed that the Spirit of Sorrow was much more powerful. With anger, Killjoy once more raised his hands. This time, the thick black clouds seeped out of his palms twice as fast as before, covering everyone again. No one could move, or even think. Pain, sorrow, misery, and grief consumed them. Saturated with torment, heartache, and misfortune, it seemed they were doomed.

But suddenly, there was an odd stillness in the forest. A brilliant white fog entered the clearing from all sides, and the dark cloud moved away from them. Almost instantly, their pain subsided. Staid, Tom, Snickers, Madam Robin, and the fairies all kept very quiet, huddled closely together. As the fog rolled in, a misty warmth and comfort enveloped them, protecting them.

Staid said quietly, "Keep very still. It's Mother Nature. She is in fog form." They all felt tremendous relief. Then there was a beautiful musical sound like a thousand tiny wind chimes singing and laughing.

Staid breathed a long sigh, nodding, and told his friends, "She's brought the Sprites of Laughter."

Through the fog, the group glimpsed four tiny identical fairies with large blue eyes, long blond hair, and silvery white wings. The sprites were only about two inches high each, and were all dressed alike in silver leotards and slippers. Holding hands in a circle, they approached Killjoy Crosspatch and hovered over his head.

"Silver is the color of laughter," said Staid quietly. "Their names are Mirth, Merriment, Joy, and Glee. They are quadruplets."

Thistle could not contain her relief and happiness. Even though Staid had warned them to keep still, she flew up laughing and hovered above the others. Before Madam Robin could caution her to stay calm and quiet, Thistle shouted, "Hello, Mother Nature! Hello—Mirth, Merriment, Joy, and Glee! Thank you for coming to help us! We love you!"

There was silence for a moment. Then they heard a low amused chuckle from the forest and fog surrounding them, and the Sprites of Laughter began happily laughing again with the beautiful tinkling sound of musical wind chimes. Everyone, except Staid, smiled and laughed.

As the group watched, the fog moved into the center of the clearing and completely covered Killjoy Crosspatch. Then, wrapped in a tight blanket of white fog, the Spirit of Sorrow was whisked swiftly away through the trees.

Thistle asked in a frightened voice, "Is she going to kill him?"

"Oh no," said Staid quickly. "He is necessary. Remember the balance I told you about. We need sorrow. Without sorrow, how would we know what happiness is? No, she will not harm him. She will talk to him, and help him understand his role in this world."

Next, Staid asked the sprites, "How did Mother Nature know?"

Their voices were like little soprano musical notes as they answered in unison, "She knows everything."

Then Glee added, "But don't worry; she also knows it wasn't your fault."

Mirth, Merriment, Joy, and Glee flew down and hovered close to Staid, Tom, Snickers, Madam Robin, and the fairies. To each of the group in turn, they gave a light kiss upon the cheek. Every bit of sorrow and sadness vanished with the soft kisses. Snickers giggled. Madam Robin chirped. Staid simply looked down at his feet. Marigold, Dragonfly, and Thistle laughed happily. And Tom's hair did indeed turn bright red, along with the rest of him.

With a final wave goodbye, the Sprites of Laughter departed quickly, following in the direction of the fog.

# Chapter Eight

# The Shell of Laughter

hen the sprites had gone, Tom started sniffing around the clearing, looking for the shell.

After a few minutes, he stated proudly, with satisfaction, "Success!" He was standing next to one of the darkest and blackest stones in the clearing. It was about the size of a large grapefruit. Staid approached and kneeled by the stone. As he picked it up, the stone instantly changed into a large, beautiful, frosty-peach colored shell.

"The Shell of Laughter," Staid said with relief. "Good job, Tom. Killjoy must have put a spell on it. Something like gnome disguise magic, I'll wager. Good thing elf magic is stronger, and an even better thing that you have a good nose, Tom." Thistle, Marigold, Dragonfly, Madam Robin, and Tom all smiled; and Snickers giggled happily.

Carefully cradling the shell, Staid said to them, "I would like to see all of you home safely through the forest, but I'm in a bit of a rush to catch the tail end of the trade wind. Would you let me send you home by elf magic?"

The fairies and Madam Robin agreed, smiling and nodding eagerly. They were ready to be home safe and out of the dark forest. They said goodbye to Tom, Snickers, and Staid.

"You will need to close your eyes," instructed Staid.

The fairies and Madam Robin had barely closed their eyes, and heard one last giggle from Snickers, when they heard a

the Shell of Laughter

different voice. "Well, get started, tell me everything." The girls were sitting in Aunt Evelyn's living room. On the coffee table, there were two pizza boxes, several cans of root beer, a bowl of lemon jellybeans, and a small plate of birdseed for Madam Robin.

"Oh, go ahead and eat a bit first," said Aunt Evelyn. "You all look very hungry."

She went to get napkins while Madam Robin helped herself to some water out of Maximillion's water bowl. He didn't mind at all because he liked Madam Robin very much. When Aunt Evelyn returned with the napkins, she told them, "You arrived with a message from Staid. His note said that it would take forty-five minutes for you to come out of the elf *Travel-Sleep-Spell*. I just had time to order the pizza. Now, eat, eat. Then you can tell me everything."

Grace, Jennifer, and Beth spent the next day resting. While they finished making

cranberry Christmas ornaments, they talked about their latest expedition and their new friends. But they were rather subdued because it had been such a serious mission.

Aunt Evelyn took them home the following morning.

Three days after their adventure, Thistle, Dragonfly, and Marigold all received nut

messages from Staid. Each acorn contained a tiny pendant necklace: a silver chain upon which hung a miniature version of the Shell of Laughter. When the girls held the little frosty-peach shells to their ears, they heard soft laughter. Staid had put a *Laughter Spell* on the shells.

A note accompanied each gift, thanking the girls for their assistance in recovering the Shell of Laughter and assuring them that there would be plenty of laughter in

Iceland, Norway, Sweden, and Finland during the coming year.

Two days before Christmas, Grace had a sleepover with her friend, Lenox, whose family had returned from visiting relatives. Grace told Lenox all about their latest fairy adventure. "We sure missed you in the dark forest, Firefly."

Lenox replied, "Well, I'm sorry I wasn't there to help, but I can't say I'm sorry to have missed Killjoy Crosspatch. All that sorrow and unhappiness must have been really horrible."

On Christmas Eve, it was a tradition at Jennifer's house for each member of the family to tell what they were thankful for. Earlier in the year, Jennifer had met a creature called the Dream Spider who was responsible for building the Web of Dreams to catch nightmares. He had given her a tiny bracelet made of silk from the magical web. Since then, she had been sleeping better.

After sitting quietly and thinking for a long while, Jennifer told her parents and her grandmother, "I am thankful for friends, family, and good dreams."

Beth's family had a tradition very similar to Jennifer's. Beth and her parents decorated their tree on Christmas Eve. While they drank hot chocolate, ate cookies, and hung Christmas stockings, they talked about the good things that had happened during the year. Beth told her parents, "I made a lot of new friends this year. I am thankful for friends, family, hope, and Peanut." As she said this, she threw a hot dog shaped squeaky toy across the room for her dachshund, Peanut, to chase.

Peanut raced happily after it, thinking about his own happy year. Peanut was very thankful for his family, his hot dog squeaky toy, and the neighbor's new pet—a girl dachshund named Cocoa.

Grace's family unwrapped their presents on Christmas Eve. She sat on the sofa with her mom and dad, tearing paper from gifts and laughing happily.

When all of the presents had been unwrapped, Grace's parents told her about a special gift they were all going to receive next year. Grace was going to have a baby sister named Emily who would arrive sometime in April. Grace told her parents, "I am thankful for family, friends, Christmas, Emily, and laughter."

When she went up to her room that night, Grace got another wonderful gift. Madam Robin was waiting on her windowsill. She told Grace that her new little sister would be blessed with a fairy spirit too. Emily was going to be a buttercup fairy.

Grace was overflowing with happiness
this Christmas. She couldn't wait to help
teach her little sister all the wonderful
things about being a fairy.

# The End

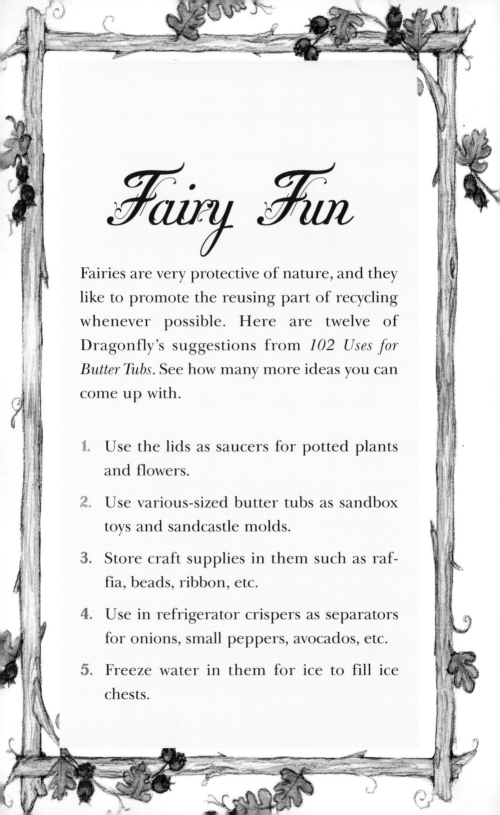

# Fairy Fun

Fairies are very protective of nature, and they like to promote the reusing part of recycling whenever possible. Here are twelve of Dragonfly's suggestions from *102 Uses for Butter Tubs*. See how many more ideas you can come up with.

1.  Use the lids as saucers for potted plants and flowers.

2.  Use various-sized butter tubs as sandbox toys and sandcastle molds.

3.  Store craft supplies in them such as raffia, beads, ribbon, etc.

4.  Use in refrigerator crispers as separators for onions, small peppers, avocados, etc.

5.  Freeze water in them for ice to fill ice chests.

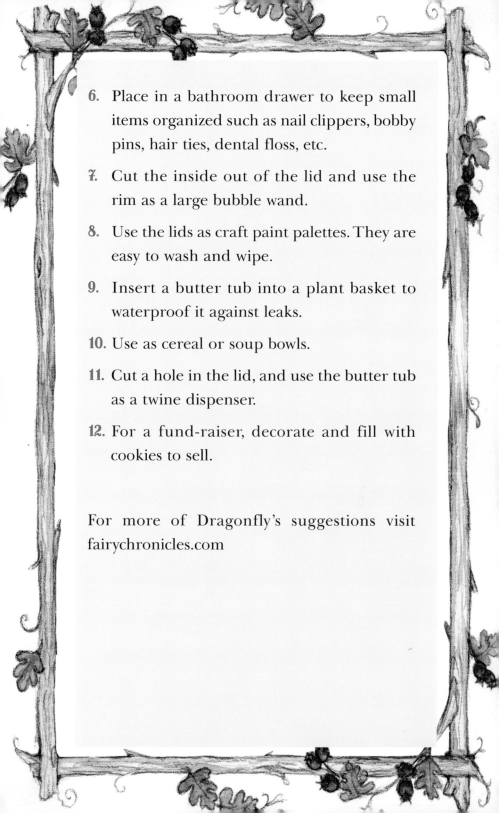

6. Place in a bathroom drawer to keep small items organized such as nail clippers, bobby pins, hair ties, dental floss, etc.

7. Cut the inside out of the lid and use the rim as a large bubble wand.

8. Use the lids as craft paint palettes. They are easy to wash and wipe.

9. Insert a butter tub into a plant basket to waterproof it against leaks.

10. Use as cereal or soup bowls.

11. Cut a hole in the lid, and use the butter tub as a twine dispenser.

12. For a fund-raiser, decorate and fill with cookies to sell.

For more of Dragonfly's suggestions visit fairychronicles.com

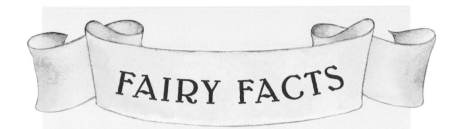

# FAIRY FACTS

## Thistles

Thistles grow in many different countries and come in many different varieties. Along with sunflowers, thistles are some of the tallest wildflowers and can reach heights of five feet. Thistles are also perennial flowers, which means that even though the plants die away for winter, they sprout back up again year after year each spring.

# Where Does the Word "Fairy" Come From?

A long time ago, around the time the Roman Empire fell, there were a set of stories that began to get told of a magic land, the land of *faërie*. The inhabitants of this incredible place

were called the Fay and were said to be wild, magical creatures of all shapes and sizes. Stories of *faërie* and the magical inhabitants of it spread all over Europe, eventually even entering other stories, such as the Legend of King Arthur. Over time, the word *faërie* came to mean the magical creatures themselves, changing with the language to become "fairy." But there are those who remember, like many writers and poets, that once upon a time, long ago, people told stories not of fairies of our world, but of a whole other world, the realm of *faërie*.

What do you think? Wouldn't it be a great place to visit?

# Why are people ticklish?

Believe it or not, scientists are still discussing why people are ticklish! Some scientist think that humans are ticklish because in the long distant past we developed a reflex that told us when unwanted creepy-crawlies (like spiders) were scurrying around in unwanted places (just like where you are most ticklish: your armpits, belly and the bottoms of your feet). Other scientists point out that it has to be a part of human society since you can't walk up to anyone, tickle them and expect them to laugh. You have to know the person for them to be comfortable enough to laugh when you tickle them. And thank goodness for that because otherwise we might all be tickling each other all the time! Other scientists think it is all because it is a way for parents and children to bond. But who is right? Maybe you should study the science of tickling when you grow up and once and for all answer the question: Why are people ticklish?

# Bobolinks

The bobolink is an American grasslands bird, distinctive because it is the only American bird that has a white back and a black front. It is a remarkable traveler. Each year it travels from the American grasslands south, past the equator, and back, traveling a total of 12,500 miles before returning home! Since the Earth is approximately 25,000 miles in circumference (the total distance it would take, if you traveled one direction, to get back to where you started), after just two years of their lives the bobolink will have flown a distance equal to flying all the way around the Earth!

Inside you is the power to do anything

The Fairy Chronicles

. . . the adventures continue

# Marigold and the Feather of Hope

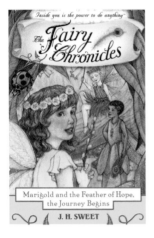

*Marigold and the Feather of Hope, the Journey Begins*

J. H. SWEET

*Like most nine-year-old girls, Beth wants to spend her summer goofing off. Unfortunately, her parents are making her spend two whole weeks with her crazy Aunt Evelyn. This time however, Aunt Evelyn has a secret to tell...*

Somewhat alarmed, Beth slid sideways in her seat putting about a foot of extra distance between her and her aunt. Aunt Evelyn was leaning forward, obviously very excited about something. Her dark brown eyes, now flashing with flecks of orange and black, were a bit scary. Beth had never seen these colors in her aunt's eyes before. They both took a deep breath, staring at each other as the room became very still.

Beth felt a tingling sensation, as though something very important was about to happen. Aunt Evelyn continued to stare at her. Just as Beth was thinking of having another sip of soda, her aunt stated calmly, "You are a marigold fairy."

**Discovering her new powers, making new and magical friends, and being sent on a super important mission make for one really exciting summer. But if Beth, now known as Marigold, doesn't find the Feather of Hope, it might be the last good summer anyone ever has.**

*Now Available in Bookstores and Online*

# Dragonfly and the Web of Dreams

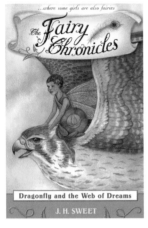

*...where some girls are also fairies*

*The Fairy Chronicles*

**Dragonfly and the Web of Dreams**

J. H. SWEET

*Dragonfly and her closest friends, Marigold, Thistle, and Firefly, have all been having terrible nightmares all week long. So it comes as no surprise that the problem is getting worse, and not just for fairies. An emergency Fairy Circle is called...*

"Welcome, welcome! Attention, attention everyone! We are here to discuss the problem of the nightmares. First of all, we need to thank the doves."

Madam Toad gestured to one side of the gathering where several tired and bedraggled looking doves were cooing sleepily. "They have been working overtime, delivering good dreams to help balance out the dream problem. It would be much worse if not for their efforts."

There was polite applause and Madam Toad continued. "The Web of Dreams has been destroyed. I went with the Sandman yesterday to confirm this. It is not clear who destroyed it or how anyone knew its location. But it must be rebuilt quickly, or the problem will worsen."

**The fairy team must find the Dream Spider, discover the cause of the Web's destruction, and get a new one built before the whole world succumbs to nightmares and good dreams become a thing of the past.**

*Now Available in Bookstores and Online*

# Firefly and the Quest of the Black Squirrel

Inside you is the power to do anything

The Fairy Chronicles

Firefly and the Quest of the Black Squirrel

J. H. SWEET

*Firefly and her friends are going on a camping adventure. But little do they know that they are about to be sent on a real adventure, where the stakes are nothing less than the future of all the species on Earth.*

The black squirrel looked nervous. When he spoke, his soft voice quavered a little at first. "I have made a long journey to be here because a terrible sickness has struck several black squirrel colonies in the far North, and it is spreading. The sickness causes death."

The black squirrel stopped his story for a moment. When he started speaking again, his voice shook. "But I haven't told you the worst part. The curse is a Calendar-Chain Curse, set up to attack a new species each month. Next month, all white-tailed deer will die. In May, beavers, and the following month, earthworms. In July, snow geese, and so on. Eventually, it will reach humans. There is no stopping it." He sighed, "It is a *perfect curse.*"

**This is a very dangerous mission, and Madam Toad is dispatching some of her best fairies for this mission: Firefly, Thistle, Marigold, and their new friend Periwinkle. The girls will have to use all of their magic, brains, and brawn to stop the perfect curse!**

*Available in Bookstores and Online*

## Spiderwort and the Princess of Haiku

*The Princess of Haiku has been kidnapped and if she is not found and saved, the whole world will forget the simple pleasures in life!*

Would anyone want to live without knowing the pleasure of a poem or the sweet smell of roses? The fairies hope we will never have to find out!

Unfortunately, the only thing they have to go on is a confusing riddle from a particularly unhelpful oak tree. Luckily, for us all, Spiderwort is one of the smartest fairies anywhere and if anyone can solve the puzzles and save the Princess it is this amazing fairy team!

*Available in Bookstores and Online in September 2007*

# Periwinkle and the Cave of Courage

*Once every hundred years, the courage of humanity begins to fail. It takes a coordinated effort from the entire magic community to restore the Cave of Courage so that we can all bravely face the challenges in our lives.*

This century, Mother Nature has chosen a dwarf, a leprechaun, a gnome, a troll, two brownies, and four fairies to participate. With four fairies involved usually no challenge would be too difficult, but now they must rely on the help of others, something that not everyone is good at...

*Available in Bookstores and Online in September 2007*

# About the Author

**J. H. Sweet** has always looked for the magic in the everyday. She has an imaginary dog named Jellybean Ebenezer Beast. Her hobbies include hiking, photography, knitting, and basketry. She also enjoys watching a variety of movies and sports. Her favorite superhero is her husband, with Silver Surfer coming in a close second. She loves many of the same things the fairies love, including live oak trees, mockingbirds, weathered terra-cotta, butterflies, bees, and cypress knees. In the fairy game of "If I were a jellybean, what flavor would I be?" she would be green apple. J. H. Sweet lives with her husband in South Texas and has a degree in English from Texas State University.

# About the Illustrator

Ever since she was a little girl, Tara Larsen Chang has been captivated by intricate illustrations in fairy tales and children's books. Since earning her BFA in Illustration from Brigham Young University, her illustrations have appeared in numerous children's books and magazines. When she is not drawing and painting in her studio, she can be found working in her gardens to make sure that there are plenty of havens for visiting fairies.